# Write On!

The Book Nook

by Nancy Krulik • illustrated by John & Wendy

Grosset & Dunlap

For Mandy and Ian, who give me
lots of great ideas!—N.K.

To Pat L, man of mystery and
a right on guy—J&W

Text copyright © 2005 by Nancy Krulik. Illustrations copyright © 2005
by John and Wendy. All rights reserved. Published by Grosset & Dunlap,
a division of Penguin Young Readers Group, 345 Hudson Street,
New York, New York 10014. GROSSET & DUNLAP is a trademark
of Penguin Group (USA) Inc. Printed in the U.S.A.

Library of Congress Cataloging-in-Publication Data

Krulik, Nancy E.

Write on! / by Nancy Krulik ; illustrated by John & Wendy.

    p. cm. — (Katie Kazoo, switcheroo ; 17)
  Summary: Fourth-grader Katie forgets to read the new book of her
favorite author, Nellie Farrow, who comes to class for a discussion, but
when Katie turns into Nellie, the presentation seems doomed! Includes a
recipe for S'More Bananas.
  ISBN 0-448-43742-2 (pbk.)
  [1. Authors—Fiction. 2. Books and reading—Fiction. 3. Schools—Fiction.
4. Magic—Fiction.] I. John & Wendy. II. Title. III. Series.

PZ7.K944Wr 2005
[Fic]—dc22                              2004024038

        ISBN 0-448-43742-2          10 9 8 7 6

# Chapter 1

"Katie, you are so lucky!" Suzanne Lock declared as she sat in her best friend Katie Carew's living room after school on Monday afternoon. "I can't believe your grandmother sent you computer software. All my grandmother ever sends me is socks. Not even *fancy* socks with glitter or rainbow-colored toes. Just plain wool socks."

"My grandma *is* very cool," Katie agreed. "I don't know anyone else who rides a motorcycle or goes hiking in Alaska."

"What kind of software did she send?" Suzanne asked. "Some sort of game?"

Katie shook her head. "It's software that lets you make your own website. My grandmother had so much fun creating her site, she thought I should have one, too."

"Wow! Your *grandmother* has a website?" Suzanne was really impressed. "What kind?"

"Mostly it's about the amusement parks she's visited. She's been on roller coasters all over the world!" Katie boasted. "My grandma's the one who took me on my first roller coaster ride."

"Your grandmother's website sounds really neat," Suzanne told Katie. "What kind of website should we make?"

*We?* Katie hadn't asked Suzanne to do a website with her. "I haven't thought about it yet," she answered honestly. "I only opened the package yesterday. I haven't even read all the instructions yet."

"Well, don't worry. *I* have a million ideas," Suzanne assured Katie.

Katie sighed. There was no way she could

talk Suzanne out of this now. Once Suzanne decided she was going to do something, she did it.

But that was okay, actually. It could be kind of fun to work on a website with Suzanne. Now that the girls were in different classes, they didn't get to spend a lot of time together.

"Actually, building a website sounds like fun," Katie agreed.

"Let's get started," Suzanne squealed as she reached for the box on the computer table.

Katie frowned. "Don't you think we should come up with an idea for our website first?" she asked her.

"Oh, that's easy," Suzanne replied. "We'll do a fashion site."

"A *fashion* site?" Katie didn't sound very excited.

"Sure," Suzanne continued. "We'll tell people what's in style."

"Why would anyone listen to what two

fourth-grade girls think about fashion?" Katie asked.

"Because *one* of those two girls is me!" Suzanne said. "No one at Cherrydale Elementary School knows more about fashion than I do."

Katie sighed. *Suzanne is such a show-off.*

"How about a website that helps animals?" Katie suggested. "Maybe we could work with the animal shelter and post pictures of dogs and cats that need to be adopted."

Katie loved the Cherrydale Animal Shelter. That was where she'd gotten her cocker spaniel, Pepper. She reached down and gave her dog a pat on the head. He looked up at her and wagged his stubby tail.

Suzanne didn't have any pets. "The shelter has its own website," she stated. "I think a fashion site is a *much* better idea. We could post photos of me modeling all kinds of outfits."

Katie frowned. "And what would *I* do?"

"You'd take the pictures of me," Suzanne said.

"That doesn't sound like a lot of fun," Katie said.

"You can't be the model, Katie," Suzanne said. "You haven't taken any modeling classes like I have."

"I don't want to do a fashion website at all," Katie insisted.

"Well, I do," Suzanne replied just as firmly.

Katie was getting very angry. Suzanne was taking over everything. "It's my computer software," Katie reminded her. "Don't you think *I* should get to decide what kind of website we make?"

Suzanne glared at her. "You're not a very good sharer, Katie," she declared.

"I am too," Katie argued back.

"No, you're not," Suzanne said. "You want everything your own way."

Katie was shocked. That was exactly how Suzanne was acting.

"I would share my grandma's gifts with *you*," Suzanne continued.

Katie frowned. *Big deal.* Why would she want a pair of plain wool socks anyway?

Suddenly, doing a website with Suzanne didn't seem like such a good idea after all. It was just going to make them fight.

Just then, Katie's mom came into the room. "Would you girls like some chocolate-chip cookies?" Mrs. Carew asked.

"You bet!" Suzanne said, forgetting all about the website for the moment.

*Phew.* Katie had avoided another fight with Suzanne. For a little while, anyway.

# Chapter 2

The girls followed Mrs. Carew into the kitchen and sat down at the table.

"So, did you have a good day today?" Katie's mom asked them.

"Yeah!" Katie exclaimed. "Mr. Guthrie gave us the best news! Nellie Farrow is coming to our school!"

"Nellie Farrow, the author?" Mrs. Carew asked. "That *is* exciting."

"Ms. Sweet told our class that, too," Suzanne said between bites of her cookie. "She said we're going to get to read the new book before anyone else."

"The whole fourth grade is going to do

that. Not just your class," Katie told her. "And it was *Mr. Guthrie* who got us the books. He knows someone who works at the publishing company. His friend is the one who sent us the books. We're getting them before the stores do!"

Suzanne shrugged and ate another cookie.

"The book is called *Only Orangutans Hang from Trees*," Katie told her mother.

"I know," Mrs. Carew said. "We're getting a whole carton of them delivered to the store next week. It's supposed to be a very funny book."

Katie smiled proudly. Her mom worked at the Book Nook bookstore in the Cherrydale Mall. She knew tons about children's books.

"We're supposed to start reading it right away. That way we can be finished when Nellie Farrow comes to school on Friday." Katie smiled excitedly. "I can't wait to meet her. She's a real writer. That's what I want to be when I grow up."

"I thought you wanted to be a dog trainer," Suzanne said.

"*I* thought you wanted to be a chef," Katie's mother added.

"I do," Katie told them. "And a teacher, too. I could do all those things."

Her mother laughed. "You'll be a dog trainer, who's also a teacher and a chef *and* who writes books. Wow. When will you sleep?"

"I haven't figured that out yet," Katie said with a giggle.

"You have time before you're all grown up," Mrs. Carew told her daughter. "Right now, you girls should start on homework. Why don't you go read for a while?"

"That's a good idea," Katie agreed.

Suzanne didn't say anything. She just shoved the last cookie in her mouth and washed it down with the rest of her milk.

"You go ahead," Mrs. Carew said, picking up the empty plate. "I'll clean up."

"Thanks, Mom," Katie said as she and Suzanne left the room.

"Thanks, Mrs. Carew," Suzanne echoed.

✕  ✕  ✕

"Let's read for half an hour," Katie suggested as she and Suzanne walked into her room.

"Are you kidding?" Suzanne asked her. "We can't read now. We have more important things to do. We've got to get going on our website."

*Here we go again,* Katie thought.

"We don't have to do that today," Katie replied.

"Sure we do," Suzanne said. "The sooner we get our site up and running, the sooner we'll be famous."

"Famous? Us?" Katie asked. "How?"

"Think of all the people who will visit our

site. They'll read about us and see pictures of me in all my cool clothes," Suzanne explained.

"I don't want to do the fashion site," Katie reminded her.

"Well, whatever website we come up with, I'm sure thousands of people will visit it. And then they'll recognize our names," Suzanne told her excitedly. "We'll be famous, and all my wishes will come true!"

Katie gulped. Wishes could be big trouble. Katie knew that better than anyone. That's because one of *her* wishes had come true!

Katie's troubles with wishes all started one day at the beginning of third grade. Katie had lost the football game for her team, ruined her favorite pair of pants, and let out a big burp in front of the whole class. That night, Katie had wished she could be anyone but herself.

There must have been a shooting star overhead when she made that wish, because the very next day the magic wind came.

The magic wind was a wild tornado that

blew just around Katie. It was so powerful that every time it came, it turned her into somebody else! Katie never knew when the wind would arrive. But when it did, her whole world turned upside down . . . *switcheroo*!

The first time the magic wind came, it turned Katie into Speedy, her third-grade class's pet hamster! Katie escaped from the hamster cage and wound up in the boys' locker room! Good thing the magic wind turned Katie back into herself before the boys found out a girl had been in there!

The magic wind came back again and again after that. It changed her into all different people—Lucille, the lunch lady; Mr. Kane, the school principal; and even Katie's third-grade teacher, super-strict Mrs. Derkman.

One time the magic wind turned Katie into her pal Emma Weber. That was awful. Katie lost Emma's twin baby brothers! It was a good thing she found them before Emma's mom returned from the market.

But that wasn't nearly as bad as the time the magic wind turned Katie into Suzanne right in the middle of her best friend's big modeling show. Katie didn't know how to walk in high heels or twirl around on the stage. Even worse, she'd put Suzanne's pants on backward! It was a good thing Suzanne never figured out what had really happened that day.

In fact, nobody but Katie knew about the magic wind. She figured no one would believe her even if she told them. Katie wouldn't have believed it either, if it didn't keep happening to her.

"So, when can we start taking pictures of me?" Suzanne demanded, interrupting Katie's thoughts.

Katie frowned. She really didn't want to do a fashion site. But Suzanne was never going to give in. She never did.

Then, suddenly, Katie got a great idea. "I know a way we could both be happy. We could do a fashion site, where we also tell people not to wear fur. And maybe I could say something about what it's like to be a vegetarian."

Suzanne considered that for a moment. "That's not a bad idea," she said as she picked up a paper and pencil. "Let's write down all the things we could talk about and take pictures of."

"Aren't we going to read *Only Orangutans Hang from Trees*?" Katie reminded her.

"Later," Suzanne insisted. "I'm already making a list of the outfits I want to put together."

"But . . ."

"Come on, Katie," Suzanne urged. "It's only Monday. We have lots of time until Nellie Farrow's visit. Besides, the sooner we do this website, the sooner you can save some animals."

Katie pulled out a piece of paper and a pencil, too. Suzanne was right. It was a long time until Friday. They had plenty of time to read. She wanted to start saving animals now!

# Chapter 3

"Isn't Nellie Farrow's book funny, Katie?" Emma Weber asked as the girls entered class 4A on Tuesday morning. "I loved the part when they're on the island and the boy jumps so high that he can see over the clouds."

"That wasn't nearly as funny as when the gym teacher made all the kids climb the ropes," Kevin Camilleri insisted. "It was hysterical when the girl couldn't get down."

Emma frowned. "I felt kind of bad for her," she said.

"Yeah, but then the jumping boy leaps up and saves her," Kevin reminded Emma. He turned to Katie. "What's your favorite part so far?"

Katie didn't want to let her friends know that she hadn't even started the book. "I like the cover," she said finally. She didn't mention that she hadn't gotten *past* the cover yet.

"The cover?" Kevin said. "It's just an orangutan in a tree."

"I know," Katie said. "But he's a very funny-looking orangutan."

"You love anything with animals," Kevin said.

"Of course I do," Katie agreed. "In fact, Suzanne and I are starting a website to tell people not to wear fur and to be vegetarians."

Okay, so that wasn't completely true. But Katie was *hoping* that was how the website would turn out.

"Your own website, wow!" Emma W. exclaimed. "That's so cool."

"Okay, folks, take a seat," Mr. Guthrie interrupted the kids' conversation. "It's time to start our learning adventure."

The kids plopped down in their beanbag

chairs and took out their notebooks.

"Today I want to tell you all about a lumberjack who became famous way back in the 1800s," Mr. G. said.

"What's a lumberjack?" Andy Epstein asked.

"A lumberjack is someone who makes his living cutting down trees in the forest," Mr. G. explained. "Now, this lumberjack's name was Paul Bunyan. He was the biggest, strongest lumberjack ever. He was so big that when he was born, it took five storks to fly him to his mother."

Emma W. raised her hand. "That can't be right, Mr. G.," she said. "Storks don't bring babies."

Mr. G. didn't answer her. He just kept talking about Paul Bunyan.

Katie looked at him strangely. That was weird. Mr. G. always stopped to answer questions. But today . . .

"One day, Paul met a giant blue ox," the

teacher continued. "He named her Babe. Babe was so big, it took a crow a full day to fly from the tip of one of her horns to the other."

*A blue ox?* Katie thought to herself. *I never saw one of them in my animal books.*

"Paul was really smart," Mr. G. told the class. "One year, when there weren't enough lumberjacks to do all the work, he brought in giant ants to help out. The ants weighed two hundred pounds apiece and could do the work of fifty men!"

"I wouldn't want to be at a picnic with *those* ants," Kadeem Carter joked.

Mr. G. laughed. "Me neither," he agreed. "But they sure were a help to Paul Bunyan. Of course, even Paul made mistakes. Like one summer when there were too many mosquitoes in the woods. Paul went and got special bumblebees to destroy them. Unfortunately, the bumblebees *liked* the mosquitoes. And that made things much worse. Their babies, the bee-squitoes, had stingers on both ends."

"Now I *know* you're kidding," Emma Stavros told Mr. Guthrie. "That's impossible."

"There's no such thing as giant, two-hundred pound ants," Emma W. said. "Or bee-squitoes."

"Or giant blue oxen," Katie added.

"No," Mr. G. admitted. "And there was no Paul Bunyan, either. He was a character made up by lumberjacks who lived in the American wilderness."

"Too bad they didn't have Spider-Man back then," Kadeem said. "Spiders eat mosquitoes!"

"Paul Bunyan was a superhero to the lumberjacks, just like Spider-Man, Batman, and Superman are superheroes to you," Mr. G. explained. "The stories the lumberjacks made up about him were called tall tales. They were about a superhuman person who solved his problems in a funny way."

"Like the boy in *Only Orangutans Hang from Trees*," Kevin pointed out. "Nobody can *really* jump that high!"

"Exactly!" Mr. G. agreed.

"Those Paul Bunyan stories are really cool!" George Brennan exclaimed. "Do you know any more tall tales?"

Mr. Guthrie shook his head. "I don't know any others . . . at least not yet. But I will on Thursday."

The kids all looked confused.

"That's because on Thursday, you're all going to read your own tall tales to the class," Mr. Guthrie continued. "I want each of you to create your own character and write a tall tale about him or her."

"Oh, wow!" Kadeem exclaimed. "Cool."

"I'm going to write about a guy who plants tomato seeds all over the world," Kevin thought out loud.

Katie giggled. That made sense. Kevin was the tomato-eating king of the fourth grade.

"I could make up a guy who tells jokes that are so funny, all the wars in the world stop because the soldiers are laughing too hard to fight," George said.

"How about a story about a mom who has a hundred kids, and they start their own country?" Emma W. suggested.

"Sounds like *your* house," Mandy Banks teased.

"We only have five kids," Emma W. reminded her with a laugh.

Everyone in class 4A was excited about the tall-tales project. They couldn't wait to get started!

# Chapter 4

"Katie! Wait up!" Suzanne shouted as she spotted Katie leaving the school later that day.

Katie stopped and turned around. "Hey, Suzanne!" she called. "What's up?"

Suzanne raced up to Katie. "My mom said we could borrow her digital camera—if we took the pictures at my house," she said, taking a deep breath.

Katie had no idea what Suzanne was talking about. "Huh?"

"You know. The *pictures*," Suzanne said. "For our fashion website."

"You mean our fashion *and animal-rights* website," Katie corrected her.

Suzanne put her hands on her hips. "Whatever," Suzanne said. "Anyway, why don't we work at my house today?"

"I can't," Katie told her. "I have homework to do."

"So do I," Suzanne said. She made a face. "*Math*. I'm in no hurry to get started."

"Well, I am," Katie said. "Mr. G. wants us to write a tall tale. I have to work on it. It's due on Thursday."

"Thursday?" Suzanne asked. "That's not until the day after tomorrow."

"But I have to come up with a character and a story and . . ."

"That won't take you long," Suzanne assured her. "You can do it tomorrow after your cooking class."

"I don't know, Suzanne . . ." Katie began.

Suzanne looked at her. "My mom said we could try making some of your vegetarian recipes in our kitchen," she said. "Then we could take pictures of the food for the website.

Just think of all the animals you could save if people ate vegetables."

Katie thought about that. It was an important thing for her to do. "Okay," she said finally.

The girls began to walk in the direction of Suzanne's house. But before they could get very far, Katie stopped again. "Wait a minute," she said suddenly. "I still have to read *Only*

*Orangutans Hang from Trees.* If I don't start today, I'll never finish by Friday."

"You don't have to," Suzanne told her.

"What do you mean? Of course I have to," Katie replied. "Nellie Farrow is coming on Friday."

"So what?" Suzanne said. "She'll never know if you read her book or not. We'll just sit in the back of the room and be very quiet."

"But . . ."

"Oh, come on, Katie," Suzanne pleaded. "More people will check out our website than will ever read Nellie's book. A website is more fun than a book any day."

Katie didn't know if that was true. She loved reading books. And lots of other kids she knew did, too.

Still, working on the website *would* be a lot more fun than doing homework. "Okay," she said finally. "Let's go to your house. I have a great recipe for vegetarian lasagna."

"Mmm . . . that sounds good. We'll definitely

do that," Suzanne agreed. "After I model my outfits, of course."

Katie sighed. "Of course."

✕  ✕  ✕

The next morning everyone in class 4A was buzzing about their tall tales. They all seemed to be having a great time writing stories about superhuman characters that did really hysterical things.

Everyone but *Katie*, that is. She hadn't even started her story yet. Not that she hadn't tried. It was just that when she got home from Suzanne's house, she had been really tired. Not one idea had popped into her head.

So, when the other kids were all discussing their homework assignments, Katie just sat on her beanbag quietly. She couldn't even talk about the website she and Suzanne were planning. So far, all they'd done was take pictures of Suzanne wearing different clothes. No one would be interested in that.

Katie had hoped that they could make the vegetarian lasagna, but Mrs. Lock didn't have any spinach or tomato sauce in the house. So Katie's part of the website didn't even get started.

"Did you finish *Only Orangutans Hang from Trees*?" Emma W. asked as she plopped down next to Katie.

*Finish?* She hadn't even started!

"No, not yet," Katie said.

"Oh, then I won't tell you anything. It's a total surprise!" Emma exclaimed. "Nellie Farrow is an amazing author. I wish I knew how she comes up with her ideas."

"So do I," Katie said.

"Is your dad still away on business?" Emma asked, changing the subject.

Katie nodded. "He won't be home until

Saturday. That means I have to spend tonight at the mall with my mom. She's working late."

"Would you want to come to my house instead? My mom said I could invite a friend to dinner," Emma told her.

Katie knew that would be so much fun. But she couldn't go. She had her cooking class right after school. And then she needed to write her tall tale.

Katie scowled. If it wasn't for her homework, she would be able to have dinner at Emma's tonight. And maybe Emma's fifteen-year-old sister, Lacey, would let her listen to some of her new CDs, like she did the last time Katie was over.

But *no.* Instead of having all that fun, tonight Katie was going to be stuck in the back office of the Book Nook, writing. That stupid story was spoiling everything! *Writing was no fun!*

Right then and there Katie decided that she didn't want to be an author after all.

Writing was too hard.

Instead, she would just grow up to be a dog-training teacher who cooked.

# Chapter 5

That evening, Katie sat in the back office of the Book Nook, staring at a blank sheet of paper. She was waiting for a story to pop into her head. But she couldn't think of anything . . . except how mad she was that she couldn't think of anything.

*Grrr.* It wasn't fair. The Book Nook was filled with books written by people with great ideas for stories. Some of the authors had come up with *lots* of ideas. Katie couldn't even think of one.

Then, suddenly, Katie *did* get an idea. A really great idea. There had to be tall-tale books in the store. She could read a few of them. Then she could use one of those ideas for *her* story!

Katie dashed out of the office and ran to the children's section of the store. She couldn't wait to find the tall-tale books. If she could find a good story and write it down fast enough, maybe she could still go to Emma's house for dinner.

Katie looked at the shelves. There were biographies, chapter books, picture books, and even a few pop-up books. Finally, she spotted the tall-tale books. They were all the way up on the top shelf.

She looked around for a ladder. There wasn't one anywhere. Still, she was going to reach those books somehow. Maybe if she jumped . . .

*Boing!* Katie leaped up as high as she could. Her fingers brushed against the bottom of one of the tall-tale books. But she couldn't grab it.

*Boing!* She jumped again, reaching up her

arm really, really high. This time she was able to grab the spine of one of the books and . . .

**CRASH!** A whole row of tall-tale books flew off the shelf! One of them hit Katie right in the head. *Ouch.*

All of the customers in the store turned around. A few started toward Katie to help her.

"It's okay, folks," Mrs. Carew said as she hurried over. "I'll take care of her."

Katie blushed. This was so embarrassing. She wanted to hide under the pile of books.

"Katie, are you all right?" Mrs. Carew asked her.

"I'm fine," she murmured.

"What were you looking for?" Mrs. Carew asked her.

"Um, just a book."

Mrs. Carew picked up one of the books that had fallen to the floor. "Oh, tall tales. These are funny." She looked at her daughter. "You finished your homework already? That was fast."

Katie shook her head. "Not exactly. I . . ."
Katie stopped. Suddenly, borrowing a story
from someone else didn't seem like such a
great idea.

"What is your homework assignment?"
Katie's mom asked her.

"I'm supposed to write a story."

Mrs. Carew looked at the book again. "A
tall tale?" she asked.

Katie nodded. "But I didn't have any ideas.
So I thought maybe if I read a few, I could . . ."

"You wanted to use one of *these* stories?"
Mrs. Carew asked. She sounded surprised . . .
and disappointed.

"Sort of," Katie admitted. "I didn't know
what else to do. The story is due tomorrow,
and I couldn't come up with anything." Katie
looked down at the ground.

Mrs. Carew shook her head. "I'm sure you
can come up with something. I think your
mind is full of all kinds of stories."

"It's not," Katie insisted.

"Sure it is," Mrs. Carew told her. "You're very good at writing stories."

"Not *this* kind of story," Katie replied. "I don't know anything about lumberjacks like Paul Bunyan."

"You don't have to write about a lumberjack," Mrs. Carew said. "Your main character should be the kind of person you're familiar with. Really great authors write about things they know."

Katie considered that for a moment. "Well, I could write about a red-haired girl with X-ray eyes," she said. "And she could have a cocker spaniel. I could make him the fastest digging dog in the history of the world," she told her mom.

"I think Pepper would like that very much," Mrs. Carew said with a grin.

"They could solve mysteries. Like they could be searching for a stolen dinosaur bone," Katie continued. "And the girl sees all the way to China. But she can't get to the bone . . . until her dog digs a tunnel through the earth, all the way to China!"

"Oh, wow! That's going to be a terrific story, Katie," Mrs. Carew told her daughter. "And you came up with it all by yourself."

Katie stared at the ground. She understood what her mother meant.

"It's not right to take someone else's ideas," Mrs. Carew continued.

"I know," Katie agreed.

"You wouldn't be very proud of the story if you didn't write it yourself, would you?"

Katie shook her head. "No."

"It wouldn't be fun doing your homework, either."

"I know," Katie agreed. "But this story is going to be a *lot* of fun to write. I think I'll draw a picture, too."

"That's a great idea," Mrs. Carew said with a smile.

Katie looked at the pile of books on the floor around her. "I can help you put those away," she told her mom.

"That's okay. I'll do it," Mrs. Carew assured her. "You'd have to be a giant fourth-grader to reach all the way up to the top shelf."

"Hey, that's a pretty good idea for a tall tale," Katie said. "Maybe you should write it."

Mrs. Carew laughed. "I think one writer in the family is enough."

# Chapter 6

On Thursday morning, Katie proudly placed her tall tale in the purple, black, and yellow homework box that was perched on one of the cabinets in the corner of class 4A. She couldn't wait to read her story to the class. She knew they would love it.

But Mr. Guthrie had other plans. "We'll present our stories after lunch," he told the class. "Right now, we have to get ready for Nellie Farrow's visit tomorrow. After her speech in the auditorium, she's going to come see the fourth-grade classrooms."

"Are we going to make a big banner that says 'Welcome Nellie'?" Emma W. asked.

Mr. Guthrie shook his head. "Ms. Sweet's class is already doing that."

"Oh," Emma S. sighed. "That would have been fun."

"It would have," Mr. G. agreed. "But I have something just as exciting planned for our classroom." He pointed to the big plastic trees that were standing in the four corners of the room.

Katie hadn't even noticed that they were there. Weird things were always popping up in Mr. G.'s classroom. The trees seemed pretty normal to her.

"I brought my digital camera to school today," Mr. G. told the class. "I'm going to take your pictures, and we'll hang them from the trees."

George started to laugh. "I get it," he told the class. "We're showing Nellie Farrow that fourth-graders hang from trees, too!"

"Exactly," Mr. G. told him.

George was the first one to line up to have

his picture taken. Instead of smiling nicely, he stuck his tongue behind his upper lip and curled his arms up under his armpits. He looked like an orangutan. *"Ooo . . . ooo . . . ooo!"* he shouted, sounding a lot like a monkey.

"Hey, that was pretty good, dude," Mr. G. said as he snapped the picture.

Katie grinned. They were really lucky to have Mr. G. for a teacher. Their third-grade teacher, Mrs. Derkman, probably would have sent George to the principal's office for that.

She probably wouldn't have let George and Kadeem monkey around with a joke-off, either. But Mr. G. loved when the boys had their joking contests!

Kadeem told the first one. "What did the banana do when the monkey grabbed for it?"

"I don't know," Emma W. said.

"The banana split!" Kadeem laughed at his own joke.

George wasn't about to let Kadeem be the only one to get the laughs. "What kinds of keys won't open doors?" he asked.

"What kinds?" Kevin replied.

"Mon-keys, don-keys, and tur-keys!" George shouted out. Everyone laughed.

The morning went really quickly after that. The kids had a great time hanging their pictures from the trees. Mr. G. even snapped a photo of Slinky, the class snake. And the two Emmas worked together to make a cute sign that read: "We Hang from Trees, Too!"

By lunchtime, class 4A was ready for Nellie Farrow's visit.

Or at least *most* of them were. Katie was the only one who hadn't read her book yet. But that was going to change.

✕  ✕  ✕

"I'll come home with you right after track

team practice," Suzanne told Katie as the girls put on their running shoes after school.

"Not today," Katie told her. "I've got homework."

"But, Katie, we didn't get to work on the website yesterday."

"I know," Katie said. "But I have to read *Only Orangutans Hang from Trees*."

"We already talked about that. We're going to sit in the back of the auditorium. We don't have to read the book," Suzanne insisted.

"I know I don't *have* to read it," Katie told Suzanne. "I *want* to read it."

Suzanne rolled her eyes and flipped her long brown ponytail behind her. "Whatever!" she said as she raced toward the track.

✕ ✕ ✕

Katie had a lot of homework that night. Mr. G. had given them two math worksheets, a current events sheet, and some handwriting practice. By the time she finished all that and ate dinner, it was time for bed. And she still hadn't read her book.

But Katie had a plan.

After her mother kissed her good night and turned out the light, Katie pulled a flashlight and her book out from under the covers. She began to read.

Or at least she *tried* to. The minute Pepper spied the beam from the flashlight, he began running wildly around Katie. He was trying to catch the light.

"Pepper, stop it," Katie urged him.

But Pepper wouldn't stop. He was having fun chasing the beam of light. He thought Katie was playing a game with him.

"Pepper, come on. I have to read," Katie insisted as Pepper jumped up on his hind legs, trying to grab the light. "Mom's going to hear you."

"*Woof! Woof!*" Pepper answered, barking loudly as he ran across the room again.

Within seconds, Mrs. Carew was at Katie's door. "What's going on, you two?" she asked.

Katie flicked off the flashlight, but it was too late. Her mother had already spotted it.

"Are you reading in bed?" Mrs. Carew asked with a smile.

Katie nodded.

"I'm glad you like reading so much," Mrs. Carew told her daughter. "But you really have to go to sleep now. You don't want to be tired tomorrow. After all, you're going to meet a real author!" She reached over and took the flashlight and book from Katie. "You want to be able to talk about her book without yawning."

Katie frowned. She wasn't going to be able to talk about Nellie Farrow's book at all. "Thanks a lot, Pepper," she groaned as she pulled the covers over her head.

# Chapter 7

On Friday morning, the fourth-graders of
Cherrydale Elementary School piled into
the auditorium for the big Nellie Farrow
assembly. Everyone was very excited.

Well, *almost* everyone. Suzanne was acting
really bored, rolling her eyes and yawning. "I
don't know what the big deal is," Katie heard
her say. "Nobody reads books for fun anymore.
When people want to have a good time, they
go on their computers. Books are *so* uncool!"

But that wasn't true at all. Katie knew
lots of people who loved reading books. She
was one of them. And she really wished she'd
taken the time to read Nellie Farrow's.

Katie spotted Nellie right away. The author was seated on a big rolling chair on the auditorium stage. Her hair was tied back in a long brown braid. She wore round-framed glasses and a long, flowing dress. She had a huge smile on her face. Nellie and Mr. Kane, the school principal, were busy chatting.

"There she is!" Emma W. whispered excitedly to Katie. "I can't wait to meet her and ask her to sign my book."

Katie looked at the book in her friend's hands. "We're allowed to do that?"

"Sure," Emma told her. "I asked Mr. Guthrie. He said he thought Nellie would be happy to sign books for kids who loved to read as much as we do."

*Wow!* Katie wanted an autographed book. She turned and headed toward the door of the auditorium.

"Where are you going?" Emma asked her.

"Back to the classroom," Katie told her. "I want to get my book, too."

× × ×

Class 4A was empty when Katie entered the room. The only one there was Slinky. He didn't seem to notice Katie at all.

Katie hurried over to her backpack. She unzipped the front pouch. But before she could reach in and get the book, Katie felt a strange draft on the back of her neck.

The draft grew colder and stronger, becoming a breeze and then a full-fledged

wind. Katie gulped. This was no ordinary wind. This was the magic wind. It was back! And it was going to turn her into somebody else. It swirled harder and harder, until it became a tornado, spinning just around Katie. She closed her eyes tight and grabbed onto her beanbag, hoping it would keep her from blowing away.

*Not now!* Katie thought.

And then it stopped. Just like that. The magic wind was gone. And so was Katie Carew.

The question was, who had the magic wind turned her into this time?

# Chapter 8

Katie sat there for a minute, afraid to open her eyes. She wasn't sure where or who she was. All she knew was that she could hear lots of kids talking. Okay, so now she knew she wasn't alone in her classroom anymore. But where was she? Slowly, she opened her eyes.

Unfortunately, that didn't help much. Everything around her was blurry. She could *sort of* make out some rows of chairs with people in them. But that was all.

"Okay, boys and girls, settle down." Katie heard a man's deep voice. It sounded like Mr. Kane's.

"I want you to give a warm, Cherrydale

Elementary School welcome to Nellie Farrow!" Mr. Kane continued.

Katie heard all the kids clapping and cheering wildly. Mr. Kane placed a microphone in her hands. "Whenever you're ready, Nellie," he told her.

*Nellie?* Oh, no! Was it possible? Had the magic wind switcherooed Katie into Nellie Farrow?

Slowly, Katie reached up and touched her face. Sure enough, Nellie's round glasses were resting on her nose. That explained why everything was so blurry. Katie didn't need glasses. But Nellie Farrow did. It was hard for Katie to see through Nellie's thick lenses.

The kids quieted down quickly. They all sat there, waiting for Katie to say something about *Only Orangutans Hang from Trees*.

But what could Katie say? She didn't write the book. She hadn't even read it!

This was all Suzanne's fault. If Suzanne hadn't made Katie work on the website, she would have read the book. It was Pepper's fault, too. If he had just let her read last night, she would have been able to . . .

*No.* Katie couldn't really blame Suzanne or Pepper. It was her own fault she hadn't read the book. And now Nellie Farrow's speech was going to be ruined.

Unless . . . what if Katie read the book right now?

"I'm going to read out loud a few pages from the first chapter, and then we can talk about them," she suggested. *There. That sounded like something a real author would say.*

Katie looked down at the book in her hand and tried to read. But she was looking at the words through Nellie Farrow's glasses. She couldn't read them at all. She reached up and took the glasses from her face.

"Don't do that!" Jeremy Fox shouted from the front row.

"Huh?" Katie asked. "Why not?"

"You shouldn't take off your glasses if you need to wear them," Jeremy said, pointing to his own frames. "Not even if you want to look good in front of an audience. Besides, glasses are cool."

"Um . . . well," Katie stammered. "Some people take their glasses off to read, you know."

"But *you* don't," Jeremy said. "We saw a

picture of you reading to a class of kids. You had your glasses on then."

Katie sighed. She didn't want the kids to think that Nellie Farrow was embarrassed to be wearing glasses. She would have to wear them. Even though it meant she couldn't see the book in front of her.

So, now how was she supposed to read anything?

"You know what?" Katie said finally. "You guys don't need me to read this book to you. You've already done that. Why don't you just ask me some questions about what it's like to be a writer?"

Katie figured she could answer questions about that. After all, she was an author, too. *At least sort of.*

The kids had plenty of questions for Nellie Farrow.

"Where do you get your ideas?" Emma W. asked.

"From things in my life," Katie told her,

remembering what she and her mom had talked about. "That's where all the best authors get their ideas."

"You mean you actually got stuck on a deserted island for three weeks?" Kevin asked excitedly.

"Well . . . uh, no," Katie said.

"Did you leap across the desert on one foot with a parrot on your shoulder?" Manny Gonzalez asked.

Katie frowned. What kind of weird book was this, anyway?

"No, of course not," Katie said. "At least I don't *think* I did."

"But that's in the book," Kevin reminded her. "And you said . . ."

"Well, not *everything* is from my life," Katie stammered. "Just some stuff."

"Did you at least get stuck on the top of a rope during gym class?" Kadeem asked.

"Um . . . sure," Katie answered. That one at least *sounded* like it could have happened.

"Which is your favorite chapter in the book?" Jessica Haynes asked.

"Uh . . . *four*," Katie said quickly, picking any number.

"Why?" Jessica said.

Katie gulped. She had no idea why. But she was going to have to say something. Everyone was staring at her, waiting for an answer.

Katie looked down at the book in her lap. She squinted hard, trying to see through Nellie's thick lenses, searching for chapter four. Maybe the chapter title would tell her what it was about.

If she could just hold the book a little farther away . . . Katie stretched her arms out as far as they would go. The words got a little clearer. But her hands were getting sweaty. So sweaty that the book slipped right out of her fingers.

"Oops," Katie said as she got up and tried to reach for the book. But her balance was off because she couldn't see. Katie tripped over the wheel on her rolling chair. *Thud*. She fell flat on her face.

The kids all giggled.

"Here, let me help you," Mr. Kane said quickly, reaching for the book.

"No, that's okay," Katie assured him. She reached out and tried to get the book herself. But as she grabbed for it, the skirt of her long dress got caught in the wheels of the chair. The chair went rolling across the stage, pulling Katie with it.

"Whoa!" Katie shouted. She reached out her foot and used it as a brake to stop the rolling chair. Sure enough, the chair came to a quick stop—right on top of Nellie Farrow's copy of *Only Orangutans Hang from Trees*.

When Katie reached over to pull the book out from under the chair, the cover snapped in two. Pages of the book went flying all over the place.

The kids laughed even harder.

"She's funnier than the clown I had at my

fifth birthday party," George joked.

"She's even funnier than *me*," Kadeem added. "And that's hard to do."

Suddenly, Katie didn't feel like a grown-up author. She felt like a fourth-grader who was being laughed at by all her friends. She wanted to get away from everyone.

But how?

As Katie scrambled to her feet, she heard something jingling in her dress pocket. She reached in and pulled out a set of car keys.

*Excellent!* For the first time all morning, Katie knew exactly what to say to the kids. "Excuse me, boys and girls. I've got to run out to my car and get some of my notes. I'll be back soon."

Katie ran out of the auditorium as fast as Nellie Farrow's feet would carry her.

# Chapter 9

As soon as she was out of the school building, Katie whipped Nellie's eyeglasses from her face. It was good to see things clearly again. She took a deep breath. She was so glad to be out of that auditorium. This had been the most embarrassing morning of her entire life.

Make that the most embarrassing morning of *Nellie Farrow's* life!

Katie felt really bad. The kids didn't know that it had been Katie up there. They thought it was Nellie Farrow who couldn't answer their questions or read a chapter of her own book. They were all laughing at Nellie. They thought she was really weird.

But Katie didn't have much time to think about Nellie's problem. At that very moment, a breeze began to blow . . . just around Katie.

The magic wind was back!

The wind picked up speed, whirling and swirling around Katie. Before long it was a full-blown tornado.

"Aaahhhhh!" Katie cried out. The magic wind was blowing so hard, it actually lifted Katie off the ground!

And then it stopped. Just like that.

Katie fell to the ground with a thud. "Ow," she moaned, rubbing her sore bottom.

"Are you okay?" Katie heard a woman ask her.

Katie opened her eyes slowly and looked up at Nellie Farrow. Nellie was standing right beside her in the school parking lot.

"Um, yeah, I think so," Katie said as she struggled to stand up.

"Good," Nellie said. Then she frowned. "I wish I could say *I* was okay. I'm very confused.

How did I get out here?"

"Um, you said you were going to your car to get a copy of your notes," Katie told her.

Nellie thought for a minute. "Did I? I'm not sure. It's all kind of blurry. I remember talking to your principal on the stage, and then . . . well . . ."

Katie frowned. She didn't really want Nellie to remember everything about what a mess the presentation had been.

"Everyone's waiting for you," she reminded Nellie. She spotted a fresh copy of Nellie's book sitting on the front seat of the car. "You'd better bring that with you. Your other copy is kind of messed up."

Nellie shook her head. "This is the strangest school visit I've ever made," she told Katie. "It's almost as though I were someone else up on that stage."

Katie sighed. Nellie didn't know the half of it.

"I'm not sure what I can say to your friends

now," Nellie continued. "I can't just go up there. I'm at a loss for words!" Tears began to form in Nellie's eyes.

Katie felt awful. Here she was, talking to her most favorite author in the whole world, and what did Katie do? She made her cry!

Katie had to do something, and fast. But what?

Nellie took a tissue out of her pocket and blew her nose. "I think I just better go," she said with a sniffle.

"Wait! I have an idea!" Katie shouted. "Maybe you could teach us how to be authors."

"What do you mean?" Nellie asked.

"Well, we've all written stories, but none of them are as good as your books. Maybe if you gave us a few writing tips, we could write a book, too," Katie suggested.

"Do you think your friends would like to do that?" Nellie asked Katie. "I've never given a writing class to fourth-graders before."

"Oh, I'm sure they'll like it. Fourth-graders *love* to write," Katie assured Nellie.

× × ×

Nellie and Katie walked back to the auditorium together. At first the kids started laughing again when they walked in.

Mr. Kane wasn't laughing, though. He just looked angry. After all, Nellie did run out on the assembly. Katie gulped. Mr. Kane could get pretty mean when he was angry.

Luckily, everyone seemed to forget about Nellie's mistakes once she told the fourth-graders about Katie's idea. They couldn't wait to get started on their book.

The first thing they had to decide was what their story should be about.

"You said you write about things that happen to you," Kevin told Nellie.

"I did?" Nellie asked. "Oh, yes. I guess I did."

"But our lives are boring," Kevin told her.

"When I write, I begin with people or

places I know very well. Then I change them around and liven them up a bit," Nellie explained.

"Let's write about our class snake, Slinky," Emma W. suggested. "He's nice and really pretty."

"Ooh, a snake. What a good main character," Nellie agreed.

"That's not fair," Jeremy piped up. "Our class has a pet, too. Fluffy, the guinea pig."

"Well, why not write a book about Slinky *and* Fluffy?" Nellie suggested. "They could be friends."

"No way," Andy Epstein argued. "Snakes *eat* rodents. And guinea pigs are just big rodents."

"True," Nellie agreed. "But this is fiction. That means we can make up anything we want. It would be kind of funny to have a snake and guinea pig be best buddies."

"Yeah," George shouted out. "We could call the book *Funny Buddies*."

Katie smiled. Her friends were really excited about their new project. Nellie Farrow's visit hadn't turned out to be a disaster at all. It had turned out to be great!

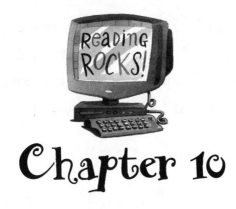

# Chapter 10

That afternoon, Katie, Suzanne, and Emma W. were all standing outside the school building, clutching books that had been signed by Nellie Farrow.

Katie loved what Nellie had written in her book.

**For Katie,**
**You have great ideas.**
**Your fellow writer,**
**Nellie Farrow**

"That was so much fun!" Emma exclaimed. "I think *Funny Buddies* turned out really well."

"Can we go visit your mom at work today, Katie?" Suzanne asked. "I want to buy some of Nellie Farrow's other books."

Katie was glad that her friends only seemed to remember the good parts about Nellie's visit. And it was nice to see Suzanne so excited about reading.

Maybe this was a good time to tell Suzanne about her new idea for the website. "I was thinking it would be fun to do a book review site," Katie said.

Suzanne thought for a minute. "That could be interesting."

"Can I help, too?" Emma asked.

"Sure," Katie said. "It's good to get different opinions."

"I know what book we should review first," Suzanne announced.

"Let me guess, a *fashion* book," Katie said.

Suzanne shook her head. "I think we should review *Only Orangutans Hang from Trees*."

Finally Suzanne had an idea that they could agree on!

"And *then* we can review a fashion book," Suzanne continued.

Katie laughed. She knew it. Suzanne was as easy to read as a book.

"Come on," Katie urged her friends. "Let's go to my house and get started on our website."

"What should we call it?" Suzanne wondered.

Katie knew just the perfect title. "We'll call it *Reading Rocks!*" she said.

No one could argue with that.

# Go Bananas!

Orangutans aren't the only ones who like bananas. Kids love them, too! This yummy banana recipe comes from Katie's Wednesday afternoon cooking class. You can try making it at home.

## S'More Bananas

**You will need:**

5 bananas

5 tablespoons semisweet chocolate chips

1 cup mini marshmallows

**Here's what you do:**

1. Ask an adult to preheat your oven to 400°F.

2. Then ask for help making one slice on each banana skin's inside curve with a sharp knife. Make sure not to cut the banana itself.

3. Use your hands to loosen the skin a little bit, but leave the ends of the skin together.

4. Tuck one tablespoon of chips and some of the marshmallows between the banana and the skin.

5. Push the skin back together and wrap the banana in aluminum foil. Repeat this for each of the five bananas.

6. Ask an adult to place the bananas on a baking sheet in the oven. Bake them for 10 minutes.

7. Have an adult remove the bananas from the oven. Allow them to cool for a few minutes.

8. Then open the foil, grab a spoon, and dig in!